THIS WALKER BOOK BELONGS TO:

_____

_____

_____

_____

Text first published 1986 by
HarperCollins Publishers Ltd
This edition published 1994
by Walker Books Ltd
87 Vauxhall Walk, London SE11 5HJ

Paperback edition published 1995

Text © 1986 Judy Hindley
Illustrations © 1994 Nick Sharratt

This book has been typeset in
Garamond Book Educational.

Printed in Hong Kong

British Library Cataloguing in Publication Data
A catalogue record for this book is available
from the British Library.

ISBN 0-7445-4330-4

Little
and
Big

Written by
Judy Hindley
Illustrated by
Nick Sharratt

WALKER BOOKS
AND SUBSIDIARIES
LONDON • BOSTON • SYDNEY

Tall, tall, tall –

a very tall wall.

We feel small

near the very tall wall.

This wall is not tall.

This wall is low.

Off we all go

on the wall that is low.

Who is up high?

Who is down low?

Perhaps we should stay

on the wall that is low.

Perhaps we should climb

on the wall that is tall?

No, no!

Watch out!

It's far too high.

It's not safe to go there

unless you can fly.

Here's my friend, Sam.

Is he short?

Is he tall?

Is he wide?

Is he thin?

Is he big?

Is he small?

He's not as tall

as the wall.

He's not as tall

as the tree.

He's not as big

as a house

   or a tower

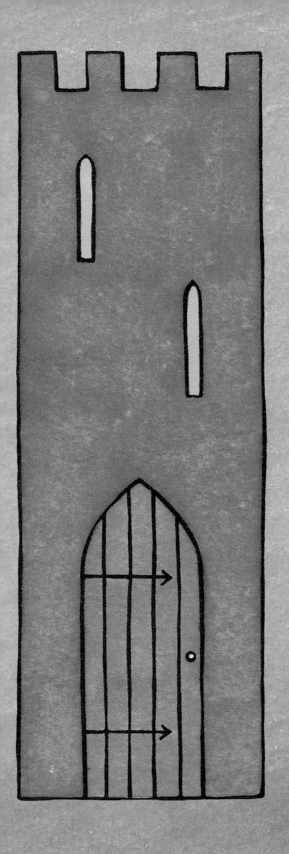

but he is much taller

and bigger

than me!

And I am much bigger

than my friend Jane,

and Jane is much bigger

than Fred.

And Fred is

much, much, much, much,

much bigger than his friend,

Bugsy the Red.

Bugsy the Red?

Who's he?

Is he big?

Oh, no!

Is he tall?

He is not!

He is little,

and tiny,

and small.

But he can fly high,

way up in the sky,

higher up

than that very tall wall –

and the kite and the house

and the tree.

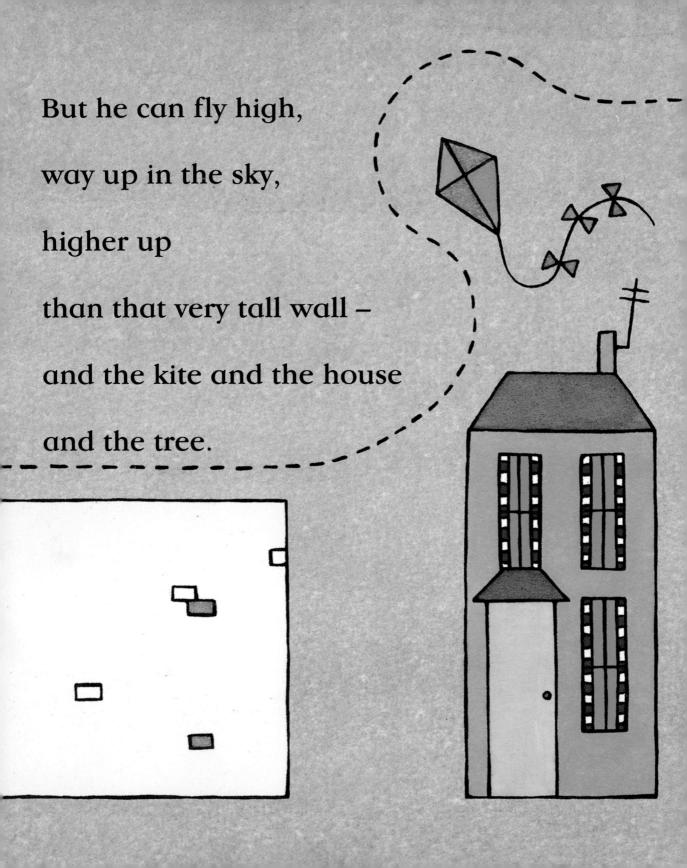

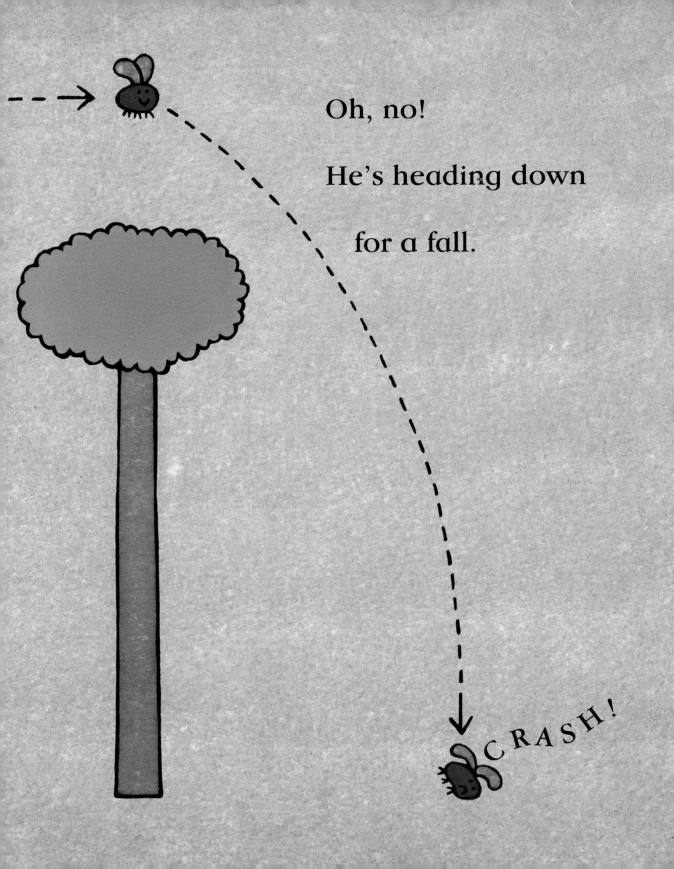

Oh, no!

He's heading down

for a fall.

CRASH!

Quick! Let's go for a ride.

Let's go down a road that is wide.

Come, let us go

through a tunnel I know,

if we can all fit inside.

Oh, oh, oh!

This tunnel's too low!

No, we will NOT fit inside!

Come, let us try

a tunnel that's high.

Hurray!

It's as high as a tree!

Oh, dear!

I'm afraid

this tunnel was made

for someone much

thinner than me.

We need a tunnel

as wide as a bus.

Oh, where is the tunnel for us?

Whee!

That was the one for us!

Now let us all go home

to our homes that are little and big.

The one that is tall,

and the one that is small,

and the one that is short and wide.

Which home

do *I* fit inside?

This one is just

the right size.

Bye bye!

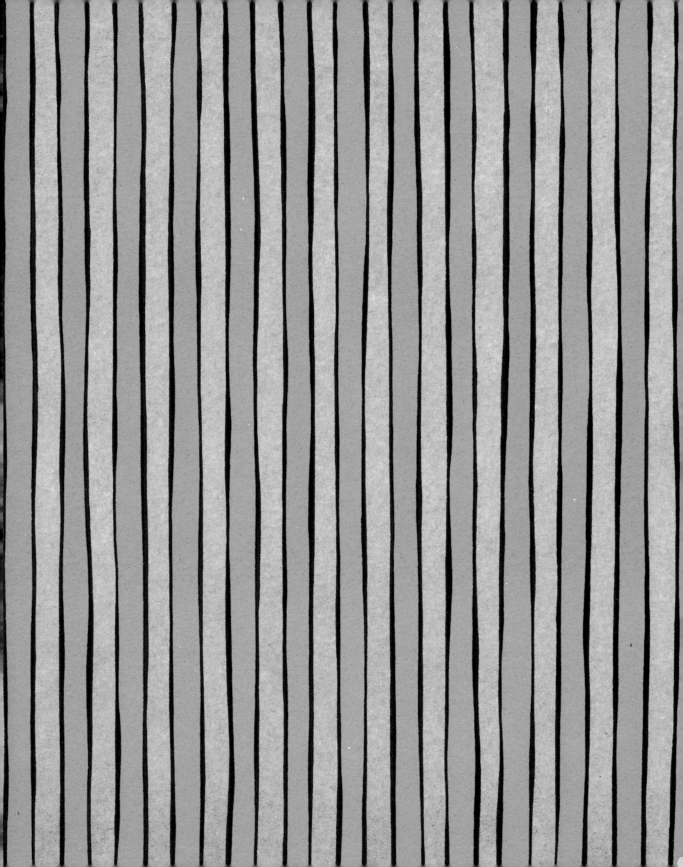

MORE WALKER PAPERBACKS
For You to Enjoy

CRAZY ABC
ISN'T IT TIME?
LITTLE AND BIG
ONE BY ONE
Judy Hindley/Nick Sharratt

There are four books in this series of concept readers –
and they're all equally zany, bright and full of fun!

0-7445-4328-3

0-7445-4329-0

0-7445-4330-4

0-7445-4331-2

£3.99 each

INTO THE JUNGLE
Judy Hindley/Melanie Epps

An evocative and playful picture book about two children's
imaginative jungle game. Cries out for readers' participation!

0-7445-2074-6   £3.99

MY MUM AND DAD MAKE ME LAUGH
Nick Sharratt

Mum loves spots, Dad loves stripes but their son has an elephantine
obsession that tops them all!

"Delightful for its brightness and consistency of concept." *The Sunday Times*

0-7445-4307-X   £3.99